The Harris Miracle

Sciah Larpu Joe

AuthorHouse™
1663 Liberty Drive
Bloomington, IN 47403
www.authorhouse.com
Phone: 833-262-8899

This book is printed on acid-free paper.

ISBN: 979-8-8230-2209-5 (sc)
ISBN: 979-8-8230-2210-1 (e)

Library of Congress Control Number: 2024903510

Print information available on the last page.

Published by AuthorHouse 02/28/2024

authorHOUSE®

Be who you are

not for others

but yourself.

Dedication:

This book is dedicated to families and parents who long to expand their family, especially to children who desire a sibling to share their joys and experiences with. Even if it hasn't happened yet, there is hope—keep persevering. Life may not always go as planned, but don't give up; instead, push through. I once desired something in my life, and professionals told me it was impossible due to certain reasons. However, I didn't give up. I kept pushing myself, and it worked. Be determined to achieve whatever you want in life and never abandon your dreams. I am a living witness that if you let your dreams die, it becomes challenging for doors to open in your life. Remember, not everyone is born with a silver spoon in their mouth; you have the power to create your own path. It is your responsibility to shape that silver spoon into what you desire, whether it's for the best or the worst. The choice is yours to make. Strive to be a successful person in society and leave your mark. As my late brother once told me, "The sky is the limit," so don't limit yourself—be the best you can be. Life is too short to feel sorry for yourself, so be wise and live your best life.

In a beautiful country in West Africa, Monrovia Liberia, there is a city called Congo Town, where the weather is always warm and calm. The people who live there are friendly and caring towards each other. In this city, a devoted, God-fearing family lives.

4

They love God and have a strong faith.
However, the couple faced a challenge and
struggle when it came to having children.

They had been trying to conceive for a long time, but it seemed impossible. After numerous attempts, the couple made the heartfelt decision to adopt a baby boy.

The baby boy was handsome with a smile
that lit up like a sunset. He had smooth
skin and, surprisingly, he was white.

The adoptive mother, Mrs. Jill Harris, suggested they name him Isaac. Her husband, Peter Harris, agreed and said, "Yes, he surely brings smiles to our faces and brings us peace, relieving our worries."

Isaac grew up quickly and is now nine years old. Whenever his parents took him to parks or gatherings, Isaac felt a growing, gnawing hunger that he couldn't explain.

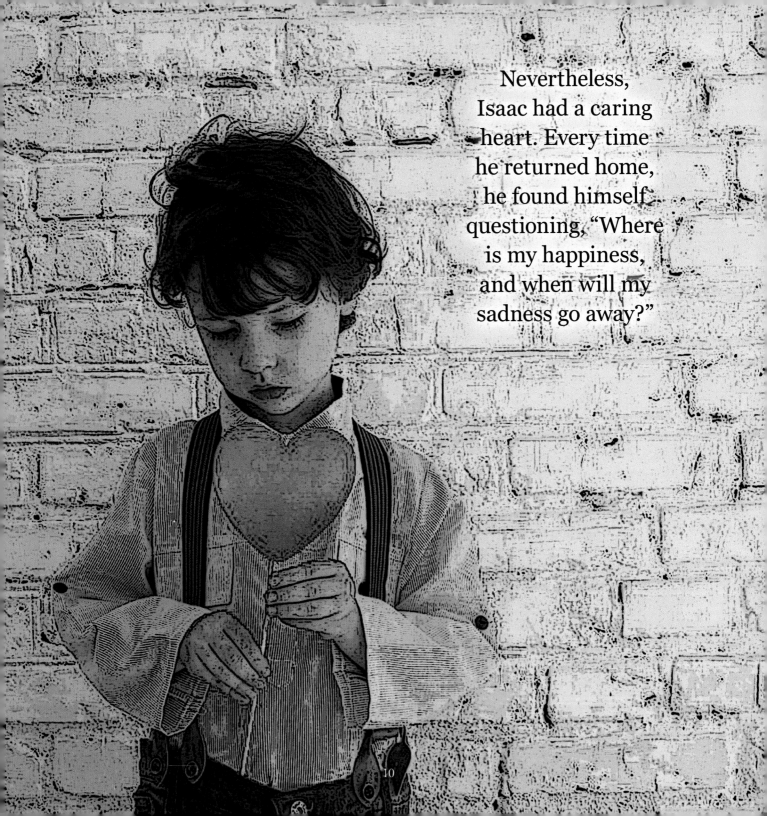

Nevertheless, Isaac had a caring heart. Every time he returned home, he found himself questioning, "Where is my happiness, and when will my sadness go away?"

One day, it struck him like a bolt of lightning. "Will my loneliness end if I have brothers or sisters?" he wondered.

Isaac went to his parents and asked for his siblings. His father smiled and said, "Isaac, it's in the hands of our heavenly Father, the creator of heaven and earth."

The mother added, "Yes, Isaac. The Lord who blessed us with a handsome, intelligent, and bright son like you will surely bless us with siblings."

Isaac replied, "Okay," and from that day on, he decided to write his prayer request for a sibling every day.

One day, while Isaac was in his room, he overheard his parents talking in their room.

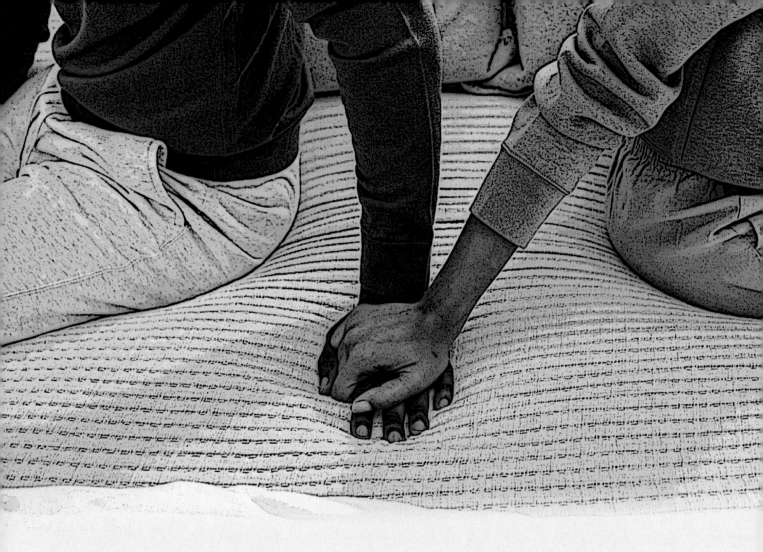

The mother said to the father, "Honey, I'm not feeling well. I feel different. Can we make an appointment to see what's going on with my body?" The father responded, "Yes, let's make the call right now."

Isaac went to his room, knowing the appointment was in two days. His parents took him to his aunt's house and left him there.

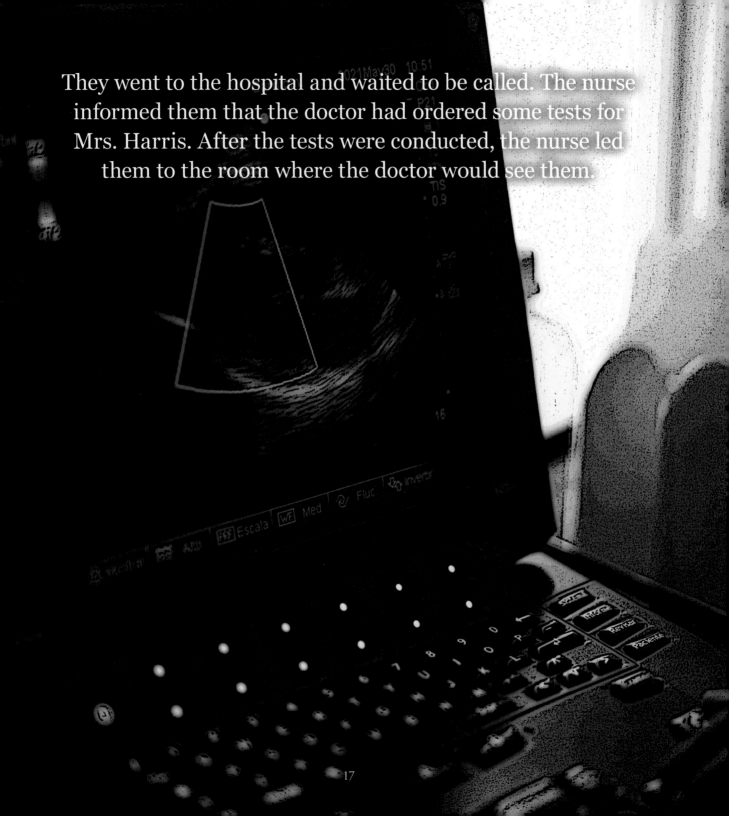

They went to the hospital and waited to be called. The nurse informed them that the doctor had ordered some tests for Mrs. Harris. After the tests were conducted, the nurse led them to the room where the doctor would see them.

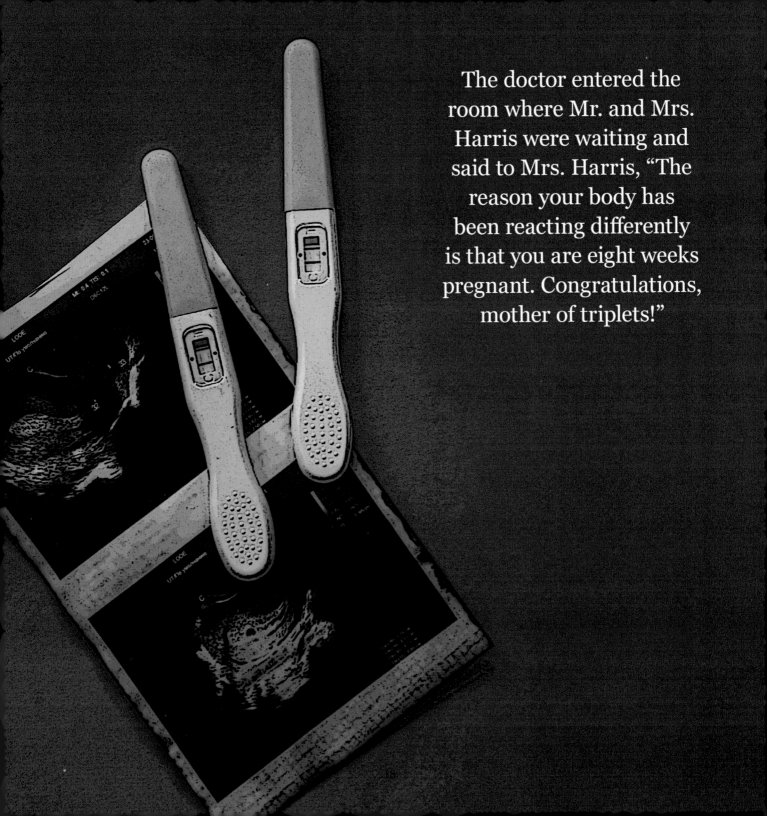

The doctor entered the room where Mr. and Mrs. Harris were waiting and said to Mrs. Harris, "The reason your body has been reacting differently is that you are eight weeks pregnant. Congratulations, mother of triplets!"

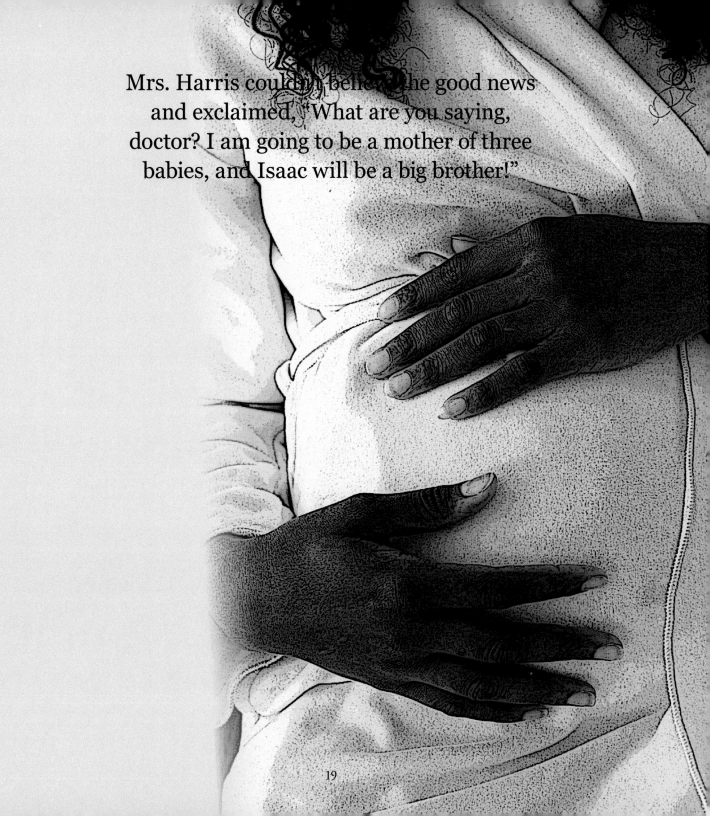

Mrs. Harris couldn't believe the good news
and exclaimed, "What are you saying,
doctor? I am going to be a mother of three
babies, and Isaac will be a big brother!"

She attributed the miracle to God, as they had been trying hard to conceive for a long time. Mr. Harris expressed his excitement, unable to contain his anticipation of seeing the happiness on Isaac's face when he learned about his future siblings.

They left the hospital and went to pick
up Isaac from Jill's sister's house.

When they arrived at the house, Isaac's mother called him into the living room and asked him to sit down. With a big smile on her face, she said, "Isaac, you are going to be a big brother to a handsome boy and two beautiful girls. I am pregnant with triplets."

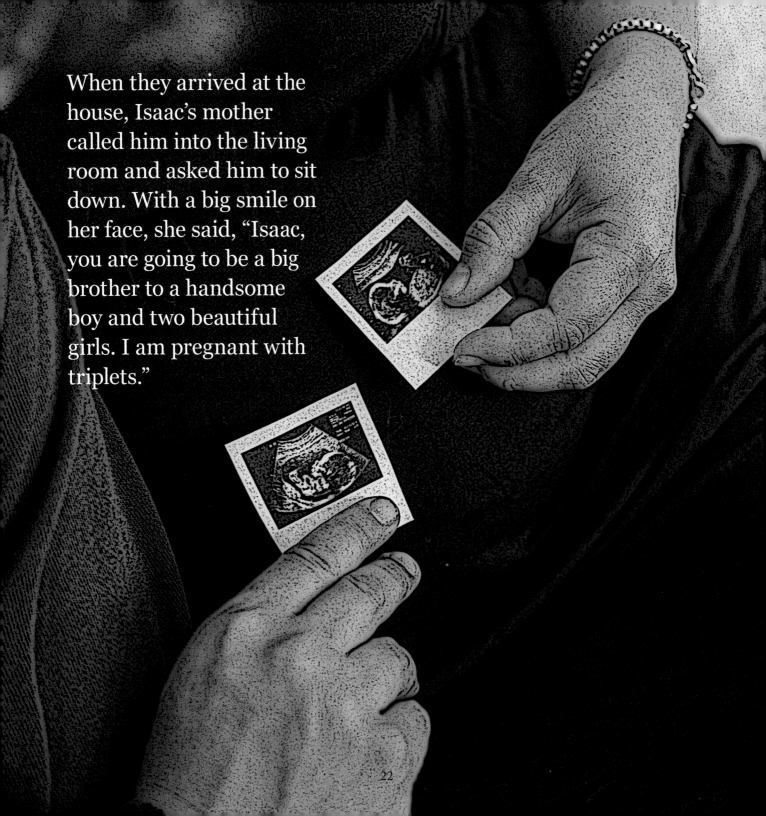

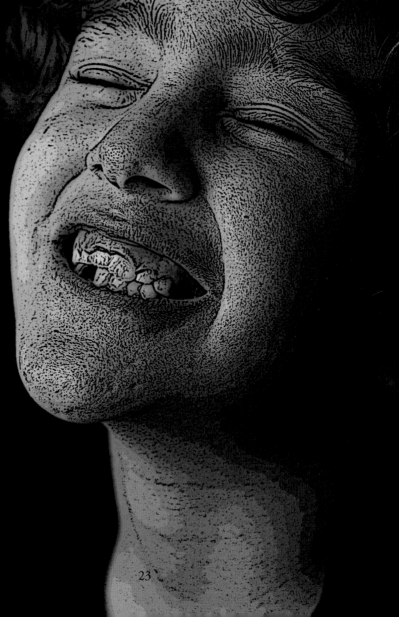

Isaac's face lit up. With a huge smile on his face, Isaac exclaimed, "YES, my God has answered my prayer! I feel so happy now. I can share my toys and everything with them.

Having siblings is truly wonderful due to the special bond we share, and they are the best company to have at all times."

Put on a thinking cap

because a star was

born to be successful.

Also will gain knowledge

and make a difference.

Parents/Guardians of Child/Children

Being a parent, you always have to be in your child's daily moment, whether he or she is happy or sad. You have to be ready for the many challenges in their lives, not only for the present, but for the future. No matter what you do, you now have a person to be responsible for, so put on the thinking cap. Furthermore, if you choose to become a parent, you are putting old things aside and transitioning into a more responsible person. Your perspective of life has changed to an adviser, teacher, mentor, doctor, and everything that comes with being a parent. Be wise and do the very best for your child or children because you are in it for life.

Printed in the United States
by Baker & Taylor Publisher Services